WHIP 4

Whip Goes To Mars

TYLER JOHNS

authorHOUSE®

AuthorHouse™
1663 Liberty Drive
Bloomington, IN 47403
www.authorhouse.com
Phone: 1 (800) 839-8640

Published by AuthorHouse 08/19/2019

ISBN: 978-1-7283-2368-8 (sc)
ISBN: 978-1-7283-2367-1 (e)

Print information available on the last page.

This book is printed on acid-free paper.

CONTENTS

FOREWORD

Whip Psy, Bobert Gatorson, and Pition Vipers were all best friends in their town of Psyville. First, they interacted with others in high school. During summer vacation, Whip went to see his relatives and suddenly, strangers known as Vips came to Psyville to rob the mall. Whip, Bobi, and Pition stopped them and the Vips were all arrested. The three heroes were awarded with thousands of dollars. After that, they built a traveling machine called the World Bug 3000.

In their next adventure, it was Christmas vacation and they all went with Whip's family to Canada. They found a new friend named Fentruck Tusker, who was a walrus. He discovered a Russian dynasty known as the Satvrinskis. The mother was Abmora and her son was Aborabor. They were white tigers. They had an evil scheme to make Whip's kid sister, Sarah, smart as possible. Whip, Bobi, and Pition saved her with changes of magic potions along with many of their animal friends and Fentruck Tusker.

Their third adventure took place as they went off to college, and they participated in a series of test rides for an amusement park of the future. Whip met his match with a team called the Arctics, led by an Arctic fox named Angus Wellington, Jr. All around the University of Harrisonburg, Virginia, they interacted with gangsters like the Sexton family, excellent singers that partied with them in karaoke and everything beyond. At the finale of the College Amusers, Whip beat the Arctics with the help of his father Tehran who got fired and needed a new job.

And now, the point in this exciting new adventure is…where are the guys, now? Perhaps they're living somewhere else.

CHAPTER 1

See You Later, Darth Vader

A scene from *Star Wars* was quoted:

"If you will not fight," said Darth Vader, "you will meet your destiny." Light sabers were lit. The duel went on. Luke Skywalker appeared with only a first-person view. He was being controlled in an arcade game. This game went on. Darth Vader's health meter was running low. Suddenly his saber was swung at the player. The "continue" timer appeared.

"Dang it!" shouted Bobi who was playing the game. "I was so close to beating him!"

"Don't worry, Bobi," said Whip who appeared behind him, "it's only a game."

"Man, I could have killed him all the way," said Bobi.

"Guys," said Pition who was slithering by Whip and Bobi. "Why don't we get out of here? I'm getting hissed out with the fun."

The guys were at Laser Quest in a mall in Harrisonburg, Virginia. It was the summer of 2005 after three years of college at the Appalachian University. Whip Psy, Bobert Gatorson, Pition Vipers and Fentruck Tusker have a house owned together. They are roommates now for this part of the story. After visiting Laser Quest, they all drove home.

"Man, that Star Wars game was just under my mastery," said Bobi. "I was so close to winning it."

"Relax, Bobi," said Whip. "Not everyone is meant to win. Let's go home and relax."

"Sure," said Pition. "How about playing Jeopardy?"

"Not in the mood," said Bobi.

"It's not too bad," said Fentruck. "My old buddy, Crow Buck and I always worked until we became famous together. Now that I'm with you guys, for sure we'll all be famous."

"I'll count on it, Fent," said Whip. He drove the car to an old brown wooden house in the middle of town. There they all relaxed and enjoyed their new lives.

CHAPTER 2

Work At the Marines

The next morning, Whip had a call for a job interview at a marine park in Aquia Harbor. After a long call, he woke up his friends and invited them to come with him on a long drive eastward to that harbor.

"You have a job, Whip?" asked Pition.

"Cool crocs!" said Bobi.

"Let's hit the road, gentlemen," said Whip. "We're about to see some sea creatures."

"Wow, just like I used to be," said Fentruck. The guys went into their car and Whip started driving.

"I got a question, Whip," said Bobi. "Do we get to work with you?"

"I guess," said Whip. "It depends on what the employer says."

After the drive out of Harrisonburg, it was about to take two hours to get to the harbor. It was a long drive through most of northern Virginia.

"Anybody have to use the restroom?" Whip would ask.

"Sort of," "Definitely!" anyone would say. Whip would just stop by any exit for a rest area.

And so, after the hours passed the guys were finally at the Aquias Park. Whip and his pals walked into the entrance and looked for the office.

"Wow!" Bobi exclaimed. "This place is cool. Is that the tank for the dolphins or what?"

Everyone followed Whip to the employment office.

"Hello," said the man in charge in his office, as the gang found the chief employer. Whip entered the office and sat in front of the desk. A long interview happened between him and the employer. This went on for 20 minutes; Whip received some papers to sign. As they were about to finish, Whip had one last question.

"Is it alright?" he asked. "'Cause I have friends here and I was wondering if they can help me work around here."

"Sure," said the employer. "Just tell them your duty here and they'll be more than welcome to work with you."

Whip walked out of the office. His friends followed him out of the building. Outside, Whip remembered what to do. He was first told to clean the dolphins' tank. The crew went there and put on diving suits rented from employees' lockers. Fentruck didn't need a suit because he is a walrus. Bobi, as a crocodile, was indeed a good swimmer. Whip wore a suit and dove down into the tank with a brush in his hand. Three dolphins were swimming around him as Whip was scrubbing the algae on the walls and floor.

"I think the dolphins like him," said Bobi.

It took about five minutes to clean the tank. It seemed deeper than anybody's backyard swimming pool. Whip had a snorkel tube for filtering his breath underwater. The tank had a filter system for keeping it clean as the algae was all scrubbed. After all the cleaning, Whip went up to his friends and said, "That's the best I can do."

"You just got it all done, man," said Bobi.

"So, what's next?" asked Fentruck.

"Let's go see all the rides and aquaria," said Whip. The crew traveled the park until Whip got another call. He grabbed his cell phone from his pocket and answered it.

"You are now in charge of the Manta Coaster," said the chief employer.

"Thanks, sir," said Whip as he hung up.

Our gang looked around the rides and searched for the Manta Coaster. Many workers were already activating each other ride and supervising it. Finally, the guys found the Manta Coaster. This ride looked like a manta ray with car seats running down from its head to the end of its tail. The front seats were placed at the head of the manta ray. And so, Whip got a chance to activate the ride and to secure the customers waiting in line. Bobi, Pition, and Fentruck joined the people in line.

"May I see your bracelets?" Whip asked each customer passing by and going aboard the coaster. Bobi, Pition, and Fentruck did not wear those paper bracelets because they were with Whip as he was hired in the work.

And so, the first group of customers was installed in the coaster. Whip announced the safety rules: "Arms and legs in the vehicle. Always wear seat belts and hold onto the bars and never leave your group while riding. Good luck!"

He activated the ride and the coaster moved ahead and seconds later it started going downhill and running faster.

"Whoa, MAN!" shouted Bobi.

"Here we go!" said Pition.

The coaster turned at a curve that led to the whole ride. The riders were screaming. Whip's friends started laughing and shouted, "Whoo-hoo!" as they rode the coaster. They all put their hands in the air. The vehicle ran up a hill, then a loop, and then another steep hill. It passed where Whip was standing by and the coaster ran around the whole rail a second time.

Moments later, it was quitting time. Whip and his pals headed where they entered at the gate.

"Man, I had so much fun," said Bobi.

"Me, too," said Pition feeling dizzy.

The gang headed back to the parking lot and into the car and Whip drove it all the way back home.

CHAPTER 3

The News

At home, our gang was watching T.V. They were watching football on the SportsCenter station. Suddenly, a news report came on.

"We interrupt this program for our latest astronomical broadcast," said the reporter. "We have discovered some strange activity on Mars."

"Wowzers," said Bobi and Pition simultaneously.

"Some people have that it can be inhabited as well as Earth," the reporter continued. "Here is Mr. Alexander Pounder." A square enlarged showing a bear in front of another reporter's microphone.

"Hi there," said the bear called Alexander Pounder. "My daughter, Ursula, recently made a career for space exploration and she has been away on Mars for approximately three days, she is a member of the NASA right now."

The reporter started to talk again showing the view of a newly built airtight city on Mars.

"Man," said Whip.

"Bleeding Kansas!" said Fentruck.

Whip grabbed the remote and turned the T.V. off.

"Guys, you know what we can do?!" Whip shouted out.

"What?" asked Bobi.

"It had better be good," said Pition.

"We can find any of those people on Mars and help them with their mission and eventually bring them back to Earth," Whip explained.

"Not what I want to go for," said Pition.

"Is that such a good idea?" asked Bobi.

"I doubt it," Pition said.

"But how can we get to Mars without a ship?" asked Fentruck.

"We don't," said Whip. "But maybe we can find a rocket garden somewhere where we can build our own ship."

Later on, Whip and his friends decided to go on a trip. They all packed their suitcases with about everything of clothes and snacks, etc. They packed their cases and put them in Whip's traveling machine, the World Bug 3000.

CHAPTER 4

A NASA Trip

The guys thought about the mission on Mars. They were on their way to the Kennedy Space Center down in Florida. According to the map, they passed through Harrisonburg onto Charlottesville, Virginia, until they reached Richmond and got onto the 95th highway. They traveled south through the Carolina states. As they did, Whip played a CD with the song "Danger Zone" by Kenny Loggins. The guys danced along with the music as they flew over the freeway, following it southward among South Carolina.

Whip eventually hovered over some gas stations and landed for if anyone had to use the bathroom. He paused the song as one of the others rushed. They continued flying among Georgia. It took about a whole day and night to get down close to Florida. They found a place to sleep outside of Brunswick, Georgia. They started to make their own campsite in an outdoor plain. They parked the World Bug on solid ground and made tents out of tarps that were inside the machine. As they were beginning to sleep, Whip got a call on his cell phone from his parents. He answered it.

"Hello," he said.

"Whip!" it was his mother, Corbin Psy.

"Hey, Mom!" said Whip.

"How are you boys doing with your new life so far?" Corbin asked.

"We're doing excellent. We're going down to the Kennedy Space Center in Florida."

"Is that so? Don't you think they will let you in legally?"

"Not a problem. We're going to just do this 'getting in' thing our own way."

"Whip, I don't think that's possible."

"How's Sarah? Is she doing better in school?"

"Well, as a matter of fact, she is doing a good job. I hope you boys have fun at the space center and stay out of trouble."

"Will do, Mom. Good night." Whip hung up after his mother said "Good night", too. He went to sleep with his friends and they all snored in their tent.

The next morning arrived; the heroes jumped back into the World Bug and continued flying down to Florida. They continued the song.

"I wonder where we are," said Bobi.

"We are just entering Florida," said Whip. "We'll be over Jacksonville and still move down the same highway until we reach the Canaveral National Seashore. That's where we'll find the space center."

He continued the driving as the song continued.

They guys sang along with the end of the song as they arrived among the beaches after passing Jacksonville. It took them about 15 minutes to reach Canaveral.

"Highway TO THE Danger Zone!" Bobi sang.

"Right in-TO…the Danger Zone!" sang Pition.

"Highway TO-O-O the Danger Zone!" everybody sang simultaneously. They all ended the song. As they reached the seashore they followed the thin road all the way to the Kennedy Space Center. Soon, they finally made it.

"We're here, guys!" exclaimed Whip.

"Man, finally!" said Bobi.

"But where do we get tickets?" asked Pition.

"It can be arranged," said Whip.

"How?" said Bobi.

"You'll see," said Whip.

The guys went to the visitors' building and met up with a man at the front.

"Excuse me," the man said as the guys went to the front door. "Do you have any tickets?"

Whip stared at the man and used his psychic powers to hypnotize him with his magical vision.

"You can let us pass in," he said. "A psyvark needs no ticket."

"As you...w-wish," said the man as he went to the door to unlock it. The guys all went inside to see the interesting exhibits.

"Cool beans!" said Whip as he looked at all the models of launch pads and space shuttles. "Everything that I ever dreamed."

"This place puts me into being a real space hero," said Bobi.

"No kidding," said Pition as he slithered among walls and tables.

"Great icebergs!" said Fentruck. "This sure is awesome."

"Come on, guys!" Whip called everyone. "Let's look around other things. This is the first time for everything."

For all the while, the guys looked all around the visitor complex at everything they imagined for going into space. Whip hypnotized the workers to let them in for free and reason. Sometime later they came to a rocket garden.

"This looks like the perfect place to build our ship," said Whip.

"Do you think that's legal?" asked Fentruck.

"I don't know, man," said Bobi. "I'm gonna feel sick if this dream of yours comes true, Whip."

"I'm a snake," said Pition. "I'm not supposed to be involved into this business."

"Relax, guys!" said Whip. "What we need is some training." Our heroes left the area.

CHAPTER 5

Space Training

Whip and the crew looked around for the astronaut training area. Whip hypnotized the employees in letting him and his friends in. Just as they found the pool, they put on astronaut suits and entered the pool. They swam down to the model of a space station. They began training on how it feels to be in space.

"This is way better than the dolphin tank," said Bobi.

Whip tried going inside the model. It felt as if he were inside a playground tunnel.

"This is so cool, guys!" he exclaimed as he looked out a window of the model.

"I can't wait to go to Mars," said Fentruck.

"This has to be the least," said Pition. "I think the security might call an emergency patrol. Whip has hypnotized enough workers to get us in trouble."

"Okay, is everyone done?" Whip asked the others.

"Yeah, let's get out of here," said Bobi.

The guys exited the pool and later they left the entire training room, took off the suits and planned their next subject.

"Next thing to do..." Whip explained. "...is to build our own spaceship."

"Oh great!" said Bobi. "Now we're getting somewhere."

Our heroes went to the rocket garden. The sun was setting in the sky. They made special improvements to build a rocket ship. It took the first fraction of the night to get everything settled. They all fell asleep until the morning when they would build their own launch pad.

And so the next morning, they got to work on the launch pad. It was all bare ground where the ship was standing on its rear end. The next thing they need was a fuse.

CHAPTER 6

Blast Off!

The ship was a near success. Whip and his pals got their stuff from the World Bug 3000 and packed it all aboard. Whip put gasoline in the fuel tank. Fentruck remembered black powder for dynamite. He dumped a pack of it from his suitcase and he walked backwards yards away to create the rocket's fuse. He wadded up scraps of paper behind the powder and got ready to light it. And so he did. He ran back to the ship in a minute before the fire reached the powder. Everybody climbed aboard.

"Is everyone all set?" asked Whip.

"Yeah," said Pition and Fentruck.

"Totally, dude," said Bobi.

Suddenly, the fire began to burn the powder about five yards all the way to the launch pad. Everyone took a seat Whip entered the cockpit to be captain.

"Are we pointed in the right direction?" asked Pition.

"I'm sure," said Whip. "I'll just drive our ship wherever we must go."

Suddenly the lighted powder was burned all the way to the rocket's engine. The engine started roaring and blasting smoke around the field.

"Hold on, guys!" Whip shouted.

The rocket hovered higher and higher and suddenly it reached the air and voyaged to the atmosphere. Meanwhile, the workers hypnotized by Whip began to awake as the hypnosis wore off.

"Hey!" shouted one worker. "Somebody stole one of our rockets!"

The workers all screamed and argued as Whip and his pals rode the rocket up into space.

And so, the adventure was just beginning. Our heroes were finally in outer space. Their first stop was a space station. Whip drove the ship there as he and his friends were floating in zero gravity.

"Okay, guys this is our first stay," said Whip. "We'll be in the station for a short time. We'll need a lot of fuel to get to Mars. Any full urinal tanks find the nearest space toilet."

Whip moved the ship to find the airlock and placed it there by the ship's doorway. Everybody hovered out of his seat and swam through zero gravity into the airlock tunnel.

"Oh man!" said Bobi. "We're going *some*where."

"I have nothing to move my body with except itself," said Pition.

Everyone wandered off as Whip went to the fuel pod to gather up tanks for their trip to Mars. He got two tanks and had his friends carry them back to the ship for him. Whip got three more and that was all he believed they needed.

"That should be enough, guys!" Whip called to the others. "Let's go!"

"Yeah! Let's swim outta here!" said Bobi.

"I usually swim in water, not in air," said Fentruck.

The guys floated back to the ship. Whip detached the airlock joint and they flew away from the station.

CHAPTER 7

The Moon Dragon

Our heroes flew by the moon. They studied the dry seas to think about what picture they make when they are on Earth staring at it.

"What do you think the man in the moon really is?" asked Bobi.

"Beats me," said Pition.

"It looks like a dragon," said Whip. "It shows his head, his whole, wide body, and even its long jaws."

"That's definitely a dragon," said Fentruck.

"My point exactly, dude," said Bobi.

As Whip flew the ship passed the picture, he had an illusion of the dragon awakening. As it did, it opened its jaws and flew by the ship, chomping with its jaws trying to eat it. After that, it disappeared. It was just an illusion.

And so, the voyage was nearly complete. Whip could see a red marble about twenty miles away. It was Mars.

CHAPTER 8

Heading For Mars

"Guys!" Whip called out. "Our voyage is just about done here!" Sooner or later, Mars was looking a little bigger every second.

"Hooray! We made it!" Bobi shouted along with Pition.

"Hallelujah!" said Fentruck.

A while passed. The ship entered Mars's atmosphere.

"I wonder if there really *is* life on Mars," said Bobi.

"We'll just have to see for ourselves," said Pition.

By a moment later, the ship finally landed gently in one area of the red desert. The boarding door opened with a staircase. The heroes exited the ship in astronaut suits and walked on the terrain. They started exploring.

"It looks like there are plants here," said Whip as he found a fern that was nearly dry, only green.

"I see Phobos and Deimos!" said Bobi as he found Mars's two moons.

CHAPTER 9
Parental News

Meanwhile, back on Earth at the Psy family's house, Whip's parents had some explaining during dinner and beyond. Corbin had a scheduled surgery to have her uterus removed (menopause). A babysitter was hired for Sarah, who is currently eleven years old in this story.

It was after dinner Corbin announced, "Tomorrow I have an appointment at the hospital and I'm gonna have my uterus removed."

"Uterus?" asked Sarah.

"The organ in my body that has babies developed inside," said Corbin, "but after years with children I am about to have it taken out."

Sarah thought about women having babies, just knowing that her mother was done having children. She also knew that her father had lots of work at the office. Corbin hired a vixen named Christine Angelo to babysit Sarah. Christine was very nice and she and Sarah are good friends.

And so, the plan was made. Tehran went to work and Corbin went to the hospital. A while later, Christine came by the door she rang the bell and Sarah answered.

"Christine!" she exclaimed.

"Hi, Sarah," Christine replied. "What do you want to do today since both of your parents are gone?"

"I thought you had homework," said Sarah.

"I already finished it at home," said Christine. "Do you want to play a game? ...er, watch a movie?"

"I've got lots of ideas," Sarah said. She went to the game closet and brought out The Game of LIFE®. Then she went to her bedroom and grabbed her old stuffed toy dragon, Fredwick. She went to the family room and joined Christine at the coffee table where they set up the game.

"I *love* this game," said Christine. "Do you still talk to that dragon of yours?"

"Yeah," said Sarah. "I still sleep with him, too. Plus I still talk to him and he still talks to me. By the way, how old are you?"

"I'm eighteen," said Christine. "I just graduated from high school."

And so, these girls started playing the game. They chose their plastic cars and Sarah made Fredwick come to life to choose his. (He would always have the green car).

"Wow!" Christine was startled. "How did he come to life?"

"I talk to him and he always does whatever he wants to do," Sarah explained. "He's a magical toy."

They started taking each turn by spinning the spinner and following the rules of the paths they chose and so on.

CHAPTER 10

Research

Throughout the desert on Mars, our heroes looked around for research. They found the rocks that were named after cartoon characters.

"One of these rocks was named 'Yogi' like Yogi Bear," said Whip.

"Cool," said Bobi. He ran off and checked the rocks out. "Dudes! Hey! One must be Scooby-Doo, right?"

"This place sure gets better all the time," said Pition.

"Let's face it," said Whip. "The more we study this planet, the more likely we get to live on it."

"I concur," said Fentruck. "I wonder what it's like to live on Mars."

Bobi found something far away and ran back to the others to tell them about it.

"Guys, I found some bugs over there!" he said as he pointed behind himself with his thumb. "There are a bunch of insects around this big... Trunchbull spider."

"Did you say 'Trunchbull'?" asked Fentruck.

"Yeah, like from Roald Dahl's novel *Matilda,* the evil principal..." said Bobi.

"Okay, we know it, Bobe," said Whip. "Show us." Bobi led the others to a rock with plants growing over it. There lived a spider with insects being enslaved.

"This is the Trunchbull spider," Bobi explained. "Now I see a damselfly, a butterfly and some big flies."

"The damselfly we will call Matilda," said Whip. "And I guess this magnificent butterfly is Miss Honey."

"Good idea," said Bobi. "I suppose this horsefly right here can be Bruce Bogtrotter, who is that one fat kid who is told to eat all the chocolate cake."

"The damselfly sure does magic with these plants," said Pition as he noticed a bulb growing into a flower within minutes. He was right; the damselfly helps plants grow like a fairy could have done that job.

"Well, I'll be," said Fentruck. "Perfect names for these bugs."

"Check it out," said Bobi. "Like a trapdoor spider, this one has a hole for its bug slaves. That must be the Chokey."

"Hey, guys!" Whip interrupted. "I see a rover. Someone left it there."

"I'll record everything in our logbook," said Fentruck. He took out a notebook which he called their science log. He wrote the notes about what they found on Mars.

And so, the crew walked over to where Whip found the rover.

"Could it be like, uh…Sojourner?" asked Pition.

"Who knows?" said Whip. "It looks deserted."

"Well, somebody's been here alright," said Bobi.

"Guys!" Whip exclaimed. "I think I just hit the jackpot." He looked and pointed in one direction where a base was built on Mars.

"Is that a town?" asked Bobi.

"Probably," said Pition.

"Bleeding Kansas!" exclaimed Fentruck. "I didn't expect to see that every day." Our heroes headed for that base.

CHAPTER 11

An Airtight Town

Bobi thought right. The base *was* a town. The guys walked inside. It appeared to be a mall combined with a museum.

"Man, oh man," said Bobi. "This place is filled with exhibits. Look at that model space shuttle up there."

"Cool beans!" said Pition.

"Let's explore the place," said Whip. "There must be people around here."

"Lots of them, I'll say," said Fentruck.

The heroes looked around. It appeared to be a mall with restaurants and clothing stores.

"It's just like one of *our* malls back home," said Bobi.

"Suppose it is all right to breathe around here," said Whip. He took off his helmet and smelled the air. Everyone else took his helmet off, too.

"Ahhhh!" Bobi sighed as he smelled the air. "Fresh as our world, guys."

As they all wandered off, they remembered that they had no money with them. They could get water from drinking fountains around the place. Suddenly, an echidna appeared.

"Hello, boys!" he said.

"Hi! Who are you?" Whip asked him.

"I am Ezra Eaton," said the echidna. "I've worked on this planet for about four years."

"Really?" Whip asked.

"Correct you are, says the car," said Ezra Eaton.

"Excuse me?"

"Just my expressions. I get it all from a children's book called, '*I Can't,' Said the Ant.*"

"I see."

"I think we should go, guys," said Bobi. "I just found a McDonald's place over there." He pointed to a left junction in the hallway.

And so, everyone went to lunch. Ezra Eaton became their guide around the town. He had the money to pay for their lunch.

"Too bad I didn't bring my wallet," said Bobi.

"No worries," said Ezra. "Everything's under control." The order was up a minute later. Ezra grabbed the food. "Let's get in the grub,' says the cub." The guys ate their lunches and then a long tour happened with them all. They found a shoe store and there a special sale held antigravity boots for $1400.99. They went to a clothing store and Pition wrapped a neon-colored scarf around himself. Cool things happened all around Mars.

And so, a while passed. Bobi remembered that his father, Robert Gatorson, had been on a mission to Mars for the past four years.

"Guys," he said out loud. "I got an idea. Follow me." He led the crew as they walked one way through the mall and out.

"Where are we going, Bobe?" asked Whip.

"Someplace in a base at the end of this mall," said Bobi. "It's going to be a long trip now, guys." The walk went on and to the end of the mall, and so they went there.

CHAPTER 12
Bobi's Dad

So the heroes have reached the outside and looked for the base where Bobi's father worked in.

"I think this is the one," said Bobi. "It says '8021-A' like he told me before in a letter." The guys went inside the base.

"What's the idea, Bobi?" asked Whip.

"My father, Robert Gatorson, works in here," said Bobi. "I know it."

Inside this base were working men (and animals occasionally). Robert Gatorson was there; Bobi was right about his dad.

"Mr. Gatorson!" the boss called out. Robert responded.

"Yes, sir," he answered.

"We have visitors who are unwelcome here," the boss said. "One of them must be your kind."

Robert looked at the security screen.

"This, here, is my son, Bobert," he said.

"Indeed," said the boss.

"These are my friends, Dad!" Bobi explained out loud. Whip, Pition and Fentruck stepped forward to show themselves.

"I'm Whip Psy, master of all wisdom," Whip introduced himself.

"I'm Pition Vipers, the python who coils for assistance," said Pition.

"I'm Fentruck Tusker, walrus of adventure and fame," said Fentruck.

"Pleased to meet you all," said Robert. "I'm a very busy croc on this planet."

"I can see that, Dad," said Bobi. "When will you ever get off it and come back to Earth?"

"I am not sure," said Robert. "All I know is that my fellow workers and I have worked on these bases ever since I got here."

"That explains," said Bobi.

"We should be going, sir," said Whip. "We've all got work to do." The guys left the base as Robert got back to work.

CHAPTER 13

Ursula Pounder

The crew went back to the mall base and looked around at a store with an alien, who was green with one big eye on his face and two eyes on stalks on top of his head. He played on a group of bongos and kettle drums.

"Hello, boys," the alien said. "I am Sory, an extra-terrestrial from light years away."

"We are visitors from planet Earth," Whip explained. "We are on a mission here to look for a bear named Ursula Pounder, who was visiting this planet recently."

The alien called Sory, looked into his crystal ball and said, "Find and seek the one called Ursula Pounder, a bear astronaut/researcher." The ball showed Pounder walking around the red desert, researching rocks and new life forms. She was later walking up steps on Olympus Mons.

"She's hiking on Olympus Mons," said Whip.

"She needs supervision!" said Bobi.

"And we're the guys to do it," said Fentruck.

The crystal ball's images vanished. The guys headed for the exit.

"Thanks for everything, Mr. Sory," said Whip.

"My pleasure," said Sory.

On their way out, the guys rented a rover and Whip drove it all the way across the desert to Olympus Mons.

"Oh good," said Pition. "I was thinking that we would be heroes on *this* planet just like we were on our own."

As they arrived at Olympus Mons, they saw Ursula Pounder about 15 feet above ground. They followed her footsteps up the foot of the mountain and then they finally met up with her.

"Hello," said Whip to Pounder.

"Who are you?" Pounder asked.

"My name is Whip Psy and these are my friends," Whip introduced himself and the others.

"Call me Bobi the croc of the rocks," said Bobi.

"Pition's the name. Constriction is my game," said Pition.

"I'm Fentruck, the famous walrus of archaeology," said Fen-truck.

"I believe you are Ursula Pounder," said Whip.

"That's *me* all right," said Pounder. "How do you know about me?"

"We watched the news and heard all about you," said Whip. "We came to Mars to help those in need."

"I don't need help," said Pounder. "I'm alright on my own. I know what I'm doing here."

"Well, excuse us," said Bobi. "Whip, I say we let her do her thing while we do ours."

"One day she will regret it," said Whip. "She will need help soon enough… but not today."

Suddenly, a red glow appeared high on the mountainside.

"Something's up there," Whip said. "Let's check it out." He started walking up the mountain as the others followed him.

"I don't know about you, guys," said Pition. "This is going to give me the spooks and blow my scales off slowly."

CHAPTER 14

Hike on Olympus Mons

The gang was still climbing the mountain and they were halfway to that red glow.

"Great Gatsby!" said Fentruck. "There must be an alien of some kind. I'll have to put it in my logbook when we get up there."

It took them nearly an hour to get up to the cave with that glow. Finally they got up to the cave's mouth. Fentruck started taking more notes. Whip believed that some strange alien activity was happening. Suddenly a rumble in the cave occurred. A giant red alien with glowing, large orange eyes and the limbs of an arthropod, emerged by crashing through a wall. It made a loud screeching noise.

"Man," said Whip with his hands over his ears, "this thing is causing us trouble."

"Could this be a Martian?" asked Bobi.

"I guess so," said Whip.

Pition, remembering that he had no ears to hear anything loud, snuck under the monster and then called to the others.

"Go for his eyes!" he shouted.

Fentruck took his machine gun out of his backpack and aimed for the alien's eyes. He fired it. The Martian screamed as Pition slithered quickly away from the rampage and back with his partners. The so-called Martian backed away and walked deeper into the cave. Our heroes made an exit and carefully climbed down the mountainside.

"Hoo-hoo!" Bobi huffed as he worried about falling down. Suddenly, a rock broke off and Bobi's arm flew aside.

"Whoa!" he cried. "I'm gonna die, I'm gonna die."

"Hang on, Bobi!" Whip called to him.

"I'm trying!" Bobi cried as he could barely hold onto another rock as it broke free, too. Bobi began to fall. He screamed. Whip dove down and caught him. He used the magic of his specimen to perform a hang glider to slow down the fall. Whip carried Bobi to safety at the bottom of the mountain. Pition and Fentruck came down and caught up with them.

"Is Bobi all right?!" Pition called to Whip.

"He's all right, just a little huffy," Whip answered. Bobi was huffing and puffing until he breathed hard and said, "Hoo…wow! That was intense, Whip!"

"You almost died on us," said Pition.

"Something tells me we should camp and rest," said Fentruck as he saw a large, hot-burning boulder that came from the explosion caused by the monster on Olympus Mons.

"Good point," said Whip. Our heroes set up camp with stuff from their backpacks. They set out sleeping bags and pillows. They started to sleep. A while later, Bobi started singing to himself the silly song, "Hello, Mudduh! Hello, Fadduh!"

As Pition sensed it like a charmed snake, he raised his neck from his pillow and looked at Bobi singing.

He sang the whole song as he slept. Pition went back to sleep.

CHAPTER 15

Sarah in Trouble

Meanwhile, back on Earth, Tehran Psy was working with other workers in the conference room of the office. A bearded dragon by the name of Roger Klench, shared his files with the others.

"Here are my new great ideas, ladies and gentlemen," Mr. Klench explained. "Here I have the perfect charity banks for raising people's salaries…"

Meanwhile, Sarah was sneaking up the building to avoid being seen. She snuck up by crawling on the ceiling. She read people's minds for if they were busy or if they might catch her sneaking around. She snuck until she finally reached the floor that her father was currently working on. She heard the people talking in the conference room. She waited for them to stop talking. Soon, they all went out of the conference room and down to the cafeteria on the first floor. Sarah secretly followed them all the way down by climbing up to the ceiling and opening a hatch that led to an airway. She snuck to the elevator shaft.

A while passed, the cafeteria looked small like a pizza parlor. Tehran and his fellow workers sat at one table as Sarah secretly crawled under another table next to them and then got up on one of the seats. It was a minute or two until Tehran could unexpectedly find his daughter there.

"Sarah?" Tehran finally saw her at the neighboring table.

"Hi, Dad," said Sarah. "I came to visit you."

"Well, I'm having lunch right now," said Tehran.

"Eww!" Sarah exclaimed as she saw Roger Klench sitting near Tehran. "What kind of lizard is that?"

"Lizard?!" Klench said as he saw Sarah at the neighboring table. "I am a bearded dragon."

"A dragon?" Sarah asked as she confronted the workers at their table. "You…You don't have any wings."

"Of course not," said Klench. "I'm a real life dragon, not the kind that breathes fire."

"I have one that does, but he's a toy."

"Interesting, now leave us, I'm a very busy dragon planning stuff out. If you are not out of here and using your imagination again, insult me one more time and see what happens." Klench looked at his files. A waiter was just about to arrive as he carried a tray of wine bottles.

"He's not a real-type dragon," Sarah whispered.

Klench heard the whisper. He set his files down harshly and crawled across the table, heading for Sarah. She panicked and started running as Klench got off the table and began to chase her around the cafeteria. Sarah hid under a faraway table as Klench looked around for her for half a minute. Then he found her and strangled her.

"Call me a dragon one more time," he growled. "Call me a dragon!"

Sarah breathed hard with Klench's arm around her neck. She said, "Y… You're a dragon."

Klench put his hand over her mouth and set her on a table hard on her bottom.

"Roger, she is my daughter!" Tehran shouted. "You can't treat her like this."

"I don't care!" said Klench as he ran to the table he sat at with the others, grabbing his files. "I'm outta here!"

"Roger!" Tehran shouted again. Klench exited the cafeteria and ran out of the building.

"He doesn't seem to be any dragon type," said Sarah.

"Sarah," Tehran turned to his daughter, saying, "Get out of here."

"I was just visiting, Dad," said Sarah.

"Yes, but you've caused enough trouble. You made me mad and you made everyone else mad! Get out!"

Sarah cried and left the building. An illusion in her head said, "I hereby banish you forever." She was finally on her way home.

A while later, the workers had lunch and rode the elevator back up to each of their offices. As Tehran settled in his office, his cell phone rang. He answered it.

"Corbin?" he said.

"Hi, Teh," said Corbin walking the road. "I came home from the hospital. Is Sarah visiting you?"

"It's hard to explain, dear," Tehran said. "I have to rest, I have a headache. Bye." He hung up. He set his head on the desk and breathed as he felt guilty of what happened.

"What will I do?" he said. "My son missing; my daughter out of my sight."

"Hey, Tehran!" a worker called to him. "Look what we found." Tehran woke up as he saw two workers by his office. "It's Roger Klench's notebook," the workers continued. "It has the most amazing and ingenious ideas. We better get him back here." The workers left as Tehran sighed and stared at his desk.

CHAPTER 16

The Rampage of the Retarded Robotic Pachyderms

And so, morning came on Mars as Whip awoke with a message in his head about his sister banished.

"Guys," he said to his friends. "It's morning."

Bobi yawned. Pition stretched his body out from inside his sleeping bag. Fentruck stretched his front limbs outward. Bobi opened his eyes and sighed.

"Man," he said. "What a sleep."

"Any new adventures today?" asked Pition.

"If I see other buildings around there is always a clue," said Whip.

The heroes packed their things. They stood up in their suits to walk around for more clues on the planet. Whip sought one way to a global laboratory.

"This way, guys," he said. "I saw a laboratory this way."

Everyone walked that way. After an Earth hour of walking among red, dusty rocks, our heroes came to an enormous white dome. Whip knew it was a lab dome. The guys found the entrance and went in. They found an old human scientist with white hair on the sides of his head, a big nose, and a white mustache as well.

"Hello there!" said the scientist as he witnessed the four heroes.

"Nice lab, sir," said Whip.

Pition looked at the scientist's name tag.

"Ro-jour," he read it. "Rojour."

"That is 'Row-Zheur'," said the scientist. "Dr. Rojour. I am French."

"What are these big robots around here?" Pition asked. "An elephant. A rhinoceros. And a hippopotamus."

"These are my newly built robotic pachyderms," said Dr. Rojour. "They are for searching life on this planet. They are good with digging and bulldozing."

"Have you tested them yet?" asked Whip.

"I am about to," said the doctor. He went to the control panel by the robot's pen. "You boys better step outside." Whip and his friends walked out of the lab as the doctor pressed the red button that activated the robots. The robots came to life; their eyes flashed red-orange and the pen's barred fences lowered into the floor. The robots came to life. Unexpectedly, the robots went out of control and raged across the lab, crashing through the wall and breaking out.

"Oh…NO!" shouted Dr. Rojour. "They're not supposed to do that!" He ran through the crashed wall. The heroes followed him.

"Crazy experiment this guy has done," said Pition.

"Talk about a failure of accomplishment," said Fentruck.

"We gotta help this guy," said Whip.

The robots caused a rampage among the terrain. The rhinoceros shoveled the ground with its front nose horn. The hippopotamus grabbed big bundles of dirt within its mouth. The elephant swung its trunk around and used its tasks as weapons to keep the doctor out of its way.

"I can't control them!" Dr. Rojour shouted. "Go back to the lab and press the button!"

Whip went back to the lab. The others fought with the robots. Bobi threw rocks at them one by one. Pition burrowed into the ground and found some sharp rocks to break holes in the robots and cause short circuits. Fentruck thought himself alone as an adventurer. He pulled up his suit's sleeves and showed some muscles and tried wrestling the elephant. He grabbed its trunk. It swung him about and later the trunk broke off. Inside the lab, Whip pressed the red button and seconds later, the robots were deactivated.

"Oh thank goodness," said Dr. Rojour, "now I can make some adjustments and new improvements on my pachyderms."

"Say," said Bobi. "I found something!"

Whip rejoined his friends as the others went to Bobi's new discovery.

"I have to admit, Doc," said Bobi, "your hippo did an excellent job."

"Outstanding!" said the doctor. "Glowing red Martian eggs."

"I'll collect those for our research," said Whip.

"Splendid," said Dr. Rojour. "I will get to work on repairing my robots."

Whip packed the Martian eggs. Then he and his friends walked along the terrain back to the town base.

CHAPTER 17

The Great Martian

Our heroes went to a laboratory inside the base. They got to work on studying the eggs. Whip used a pair of goggles with a magnifying lens to look at the eggs' shells. They had a red striping design that seemed strange enough that no earthly animals seemed familiar with.

"It's Martian alright," said Whip. "These eggs might hatch after another hour."

"How can you tell?" asked Bobi.

"I believe that some young Martians are just about fully developed," Whip explained.

Suddenly, Ezra Eaton showed up with the heroes once again.

"Aliens are playing music out in the hall," he announced.

"Okay, we're coming," said Whip. He carefully packed the eggs in his pack again. "Sweet dreams, guys." He carried it outward as he followed his friends. They all went out into the hall and came to gymnasium with a stage where aliens set up music band instruments. The heroes watched them start their song. They played out loud. Whip and his friends started dancing with the music. The song was about living on Mars and inhabiting it.

Suddenly, the Martian eggs started to move. They were ready to hatch. They made Whip's backpack hop around. Bobi witnessed it. He raised his hand, waving it behind Whip's head.

"Uh," he said. "Whip."

"Not now, Bobi," said Whip. "Can't you see I'm enjoying the show?"

"Uh, right," said Bobi.

All the guys danced with the music as the backpack hopped around. Bobi was still distracted by it.

"Whip...Psyyyyy..." he said.

"Not now!" Whip answered.

"WHIP!" Bobi shouted. "Come on! For REAL!"

"What..." Whip answered. "...is it, Bobi?"

"I think there's something alive in your backpack."

"Nonsense, Bobe, there's nothing alive in my backpack. Just those little Martian..." he suddenly saw what Bobi mentioned. "Oh NO!" Martian hatchlings crawled out of the open top. They started screaming. The band players ran out of the gym. Whip and his friends stood back from the behemoth being built up. The hatchlings created a large creature of a small abdomen with a large cephalothorax. It had mighty arms and legs of a rough skin. It had bright white eyes, large curved fangs, and a scaly set of spinal spikes forming a head crest.

"This is alien activity all right," said Pition.

"It's show time, guys," said Whip. He bent his arms, raising his fists in front of himself. It's the battle of the Great Martian, he thought. He decided that he must fight alone. Using psychic powers and illusions, he zoomed around. He found some hardware such as a long L-shaped corner bar to fight the monster on any weak spot. He did the same thing again and again. He avoided being eaten. Then suddenly he hatched a plan. He zoomed toward a glass case on the wall that held a fire extinguisher. Waiting for the Martian's mouth to open, he approached it. As it opened, Whip jumped into it and bounced on its tongue as if the mouth were a bounce house. He used his claws to pierce holes in the extinguisher. It started to leak nitrogen. He threw it down into the monster's throat. It swallowed it and Whip jumped out of its mouth.

"Whip!" Bobi shouted with excitement.

All of a sudden, the nitrogen caused the Martian to freeze. It roared in pain as it turned into an ice statue. The heroes cheered.

"Wow, Whip!" said Pition. "You have some quick thinking just to show the monster who's boss."

"Great Gap!" said Fentruck. "I wonder what they're gonna do with this statue."

"Maybe, they'll preserve it in a museum," said Bobi.

"So much courage you guys have," said Ezra.

"It's time for us to go now," said Whip.

"Perhaps, I'll see you guys again," said Ezra.

"I guarantee it," said Whip.

"Good luck, says the duck."

"I'll send you a post card to Earth." The four heroes left the base and walked all the way back to their shuttle. They prepared for takeoff.

CHAPTER 18
The Home-Coming Flight

Whip and his pals finally left Mars.

"Man, it was fun there," said Bobi. "I got to see my dad. We got to do all kinds of astronaut stuff."

"Scary, but cool," said Pition.

"Well we can tell our families when we get home," said Whip. He flew the shuttle all the way to Earth.

Meanwhile, Sarah wandered the streets and sat on a bench, thinking about what she thought she heard from her father (that was not real). Tears came to her eyes. A while passed. Police cars surrounded the area. Officers walked toward Sarah and asked her some questions.

"What is your name, little one?" asked one officer.

"S-Sarah Psy," Sarah answered.

"Psy as in the famous 'Whip Psy'?" asked another cop.

"Yes," said Sarah. "That's my brother."

"Why are you out here alone?" asked the first cop.

"My dad told me to go away from his office," Sarah answered. She continued crying.

"Here, come with us," said the cop. "We'll take you to the station and you can have a drink there."

"Thanks," Sarah sniffled.

As the cops had her ride in one of their cars, driving to the police station, Sarah used her glowing purple nerve from the inside of her forehead, to read the cops' minds. She noticed that they seemed nice. One of the cops turned his eyes on her and noticed the glowing nerve. He was shocked.

"I think we have an alien here," he said.

"I'm not an alien," said Sarah.

"Calm down, Davis," said the other cop. "We'll study her later." That cop drove the car all the way to the police station.

And so, as Whip and his pals approached Earth, Whip had his sixth sense happening that told him that his sister was taken by the police and was about to be studied by scientists. He carefully flew the shuttle back to the Kennedy Space Center, landing it on the landing lane. Workers approached the shuttle as it stopped. They looked angry. As Whip and his pals walked off, the people shouted and asked, "How did this happen?! Where did you come from?!"

Whip knew that he caused trouble. He slowed down time with his mental powers.

"Whoa Nelly, Whip!" Bobi shouted. "How did you *do* that?"

"It's all in the magic of my kind," said Whip. "Let's go!"

"Gee, I didn't know he could do that," said Fentruck. Our heroes ran back to the center to find the World Bug 3000. They got into it and flew back to Virginia. As they left, time began to come to its true pace.

"Hey, where'd they go?" asked a worker.

"Who cares? They're gone now," said another.

CHAPTER 19
A Surgery For Sarah

After a meeting with the police, they hired some scientists to look at Sarah. The cop called Davis, told them about the mind reading nerve inside her head. Sarah was taken to a laboratory where the scientists decided to study her.

"What are you gonna do with me?" she asked.

"We are going to study you," said a scientist. "Just relax." He put his hand on Sarah's head and said, "Open." He held a tongue depressor in his hand that he pressed on her tongue with. Somebody arrived with sleeping serum and paralysis. It was a large gray bear. He took his mask off.

"Hi!" it was Sarah's former elementary school teacher, Mr. Grapestick. Sarah gasped.

"I got a promotion for this job, Sarah," said Grapestick. He handed the chemicals to the scientists.

"This stuff is going to go inside you," said a scientist next to Sarah.

"Will it kill me?" Sarah asked as she feared the scientists' experiment on her.

"Nonsense," said the scientist. "It just puts you to sleep and you won't feel a thing as we operate on you."

The serum was placed into a syringe. The scientists had Sarah stand still as they pierced the syringe into her arm. They had her lay down on the operating table, waiting for her to sleep in paralysis. The scientists then began to operate on Sarah's forehead. Cutting it open with a razor, they found the glowing purple nerve.

"Come look at this," said one scientist who held tweezers that held the nerve.

Mr. Grapestick looked at it and said, "Looks like she has some alien activity on the inside of her skull."

CHAPTER 20

Whip to the Rescue

Well, Whip finally felt the vision of his sister's surgery. He and his friends were in the World Bug on their way to their home city.

"Man, are we doing this big bug rush all night?" asked Bobi.

"I have to save my sister," said Whip. "She's being tested by scientists."

"Here we go to save the world again," said Pition.

It took them all night long to reach full speed to their home. They were low on gas. Whip concentrated on his magic power to carry the machine for them to get home in time. A force field surrounded the World Bug. Whip controlled it. Soon they were on their way home.

At the science lab, the scientists stitched Sarah's forehead shut while others studied the mind reading nerve as it was set on a tray. One picked it up with tweezers and looked at it with a magnifying glass. There were tiny yellow cells that provide juice for the magic of reading minds. Sarah woke up and realized what had happened. She found her mind reading nerve on the tray on the counter nearby and screamed. A scientist covered her mouth with his hand.

"You won't be reading people's minds anymore, little Miss Psy," said Mr. Grapestick.

Suddenly, Whip and his pals came to crash the experiment. They broke through glass windows and overruled the lab.

"Quit messing with my sister, I demand it!" Whip said out loud.

"She's perfectly unharmed," said one scientist. "We did some research and dissection."

Whip found Sarah's mind reading nerve on a tray on the counter nearby. Sarah walked up to her brother.

"I'm glad you came back," she said. "Where'd you go?"

"No time to explain, let's get you out of here," said Whip. The siblings were about to exit the lab when Whip saw Mr. Grapestick.

"Hey there," he said.

"Aren't you my sister's old teacher?" Whip asked.

"Indeed I am," said Mr. Grapestick. "I'm calling security." He grabbed the telephone and made that call.

At the top office, there was a masked, tall figure in a radiation suit, who calls himself the minister. As the phone rang, he answered it.

"Sir!" Mr. Grapestick said. "Our experimented young creature has escaped with her brother."

"I will come at once," said the minister as he hung up.

Security guards surrounded the building. The alarm bells rang. Whip and Sarah headed for the fence where Bobi, Pition, and Fentruck waited.

"We've got fugitives!" Mr. Grapestick shouted as he ran after Whip and Sarah. The guards held up their taser rifles.

"I'm trying to get my sister home," said Whip.

"This is a restricted area," said one guard.

"That doesn't bother me," said Whip. He held his sister within his arms and use mental magic to leap over all the guards.

"That's my MAN!" shouted Bobi.

The guards couldn't believe their eyes as Whip used speed to escape. It was sunset. Mr. Grapestick and the minister appeared in the area as Whip was about to leap over the fence.

"I've caught you escaping from me now," said Mr. Grapestick.

"The bet's off," said Whip.

"Keep it steady," said the minister.

"What do you want me to do with them, sir?" asked Grapestick.

"Release them," said the minister.

"Release them??" Grapestick was shocked.

The minister approached the two psyvarks. He took off his mask.

"My grandchildren," it was Whip's grandfather, Ebenezer Psy.

"What??" said Grapestick.

Sarah blew her tongue at her former teacher. She turned to her grandfather and said, "I'm glad to see you, Grandpa."

Whip confronted Grapestick and said, "Meet my grandfather, Ebenezer."

"Ebenezer??" said Grapestick in surprise.

"Are you really a minister?" asked Sarah to her grandfather.

"No," Ebenezer answered. "There really is no minister. I was just disguising myself just to wait for you, because I knew this was about to happen."

"I don't believe this," said Grapestick.

The psyvarks used magic together to hover over the fence. They all got into the World Bug with Whip's friends. Whip drove the Bug away. They flew up to the night sky on the way home.

Suddenly, the police arrived. One officer came out of his car and called out, "Mr. Arnold Grapestick!"

Grapestick turned to the police and said, "Yes, sir."

"You're under arrest," said the officer as he brought handcuffs to put on Grapestick's wrists.

"What is the meaning of this?!" Grapestick asked. Two scientists approached him.

"We called them here," said the male scientist.

"Considering you are a disgrace to the ministry of science," said the female scientist.

"Why use one of your old students in an experiment?" asked the male scientist.

"You can't do this to me!" Grapestick shouted as the cops dragged him into a car and drove away.

And so, on their way home, Ebenezer showed one thing he found in the science lab to the heroes.

"My mind reader," said Sarah. "Thanks, Grandpa. But…there's no way to get it back in my head, is there?"

"I'm afraid not," said Ebenezer. "Once a small part of you is detached, it is no longer needed."

"I'll never be able to read minds again," said Sarah seeming upset.

"You'll be okay, I promise," said Whip.

Suddenly, Ebenezer felt a chill within him. He breathed hard.

"What's wrong?" Sarah asked him.

"My heart...is cold..." Ebenezer huffed. "You must...hurry home... Whip."

"I'm trying to hurry," said Whip. He went the fastest speed in the World Bug all the way home.

CHAPTER 21

The Grandfather's Funeral

The Psy family was reunited. Ebenezer foretold that his time was up, meaning that his life was about to end. His last words were, "Whip, my grandson, you are a true hero. Take my powers for you might need them in the future. My time has run out. Our species depends on all of you. We must be eternal." He rested on his deathbed in front of the Psy family.

The next day, a funeral was run for Ebenezer. Relatives and random friends came. Tehran's younger brother, Seth, was there with his wife, Argentina, and son, Adrian. The Psys' longtime friends, the Andor family (anteaters), were also there. Everybody was dressed formally. Whip and Adrian bumped into each other.

"Adrian, hi," said Whip.

"Whip," said Adrian. "How do you do, man?"

"How's it going, buddy?" Whip asked.

"I'm doing excellent," Adrian answered.

"Good. Keep it up."

"I will."

Everybody was at the cemetery. Tehran and Seth carried their father's coffin to his open grave. The coffin was gently set into it. Tehran folded his arms and prepared a blessing. Everyone else folded his or her arms, too. Tehran spoke, "Ebenezer Psy, my father, I pray about you and say that you were a wonderful father to me and that you were a wonderful grandfather to my children. We pray thee, Lord, to take his soul with gratitude up to your kingdom where he will live happily for his moments. Amen."

Many of the people dropped flowers on the coffin as it was being placed into the grave and covered up by shovels of dirt.

Later, the people were having a picnic on tables. Hamburgers and hot dogs were served with chips and slices of watermelon and cantaloupe. Whip sat with the Andors and said, "Long time no see, guys."

"I'm getting married in another month," said Moses Andor, the eldest son.

"Cool beans," said Whip.

"We're working in a supermarket," said Kergo, the second eldest, and Luke, the third son.

"You guys should e-mail me some time," said Whip.

Technically, the Andors are anteaters. They might eat ants that invade the picnic.

An hour and a half later, everybody was preparing to leave the cemetery. The Psy family drove home. Sarah shed a few tears remembering her grandfather saving her from the science lab.

CHAPTER 22

Geniuses Together

The next day, Whip and his pals settled in their shared house. Bobi had a bright idea.

"You guys want to go shopping?" he asked the others.

"Sure," they all replied.

"We're gonna go in style!" Bobi said out loud. He showed the others his father's old truck that he borrowed long ago with a rope with a handle tied to the connecter below the tailgate.

"Here's the idea," Bobi explained. "As I drive, one will ride a skateboard by holding onto the rope, just like a water ski.

"I've got my skateboard in here somewhere," said Whip as he looked around the garage until he got his skateboard from the back closet. He volunteered to ride behind the truck, holding the rope. The others climbed in the truck. Bobi took the driver's seat. Bobi started the truck's engine.

"How are you back there, Whip?" he called back to Whip.

"Ready to go!" said Whip as he stood on his skateboard holding the rope. Bobi drove out of the garage and into the road as Whip held on tightly. The guys were roaming free. Bobi put in one of his CDs. He played the song "About a Girl" by Nirvana.

"Next stop, Banana Beak's!" Bobi said. Banana Beak's is a market that the boys are heading for downtown. The song played.

Bobi sang with the song, just until they reached Banana Beak's. It was a large market with a toucan holding his name on the sign.

"Well, we're here," said Bobi. All the guys gathered around in the parking lot.

"Awesome idea, Bobi," said Whip. "It almost made me swerve."

"By the way, Whip," said Bobi. "How was your grandpa's funeral?"

"It was uh…" Whip explained, "peacefully touching if you know what I mean. He just had the time of his life."

"Yeah, it happens. I'm gonna buy some beef jerky."

"That goes for me, too," said Pition.

"I'm on a special diet," said Fentruck. They all ran in the market to buy snacks.

"Bobi, you have come up with an amazingly ingenious idea," said Whip.

"Face it, man," said Bobi, "we're geniuses together."

"We sure are," said Whip. They went inside with the automatic doors sliding open.

Other books by Tyler Johns:

Whip

Whip 2: Whip's Christmas Adventure

Whip 3: Whip's Extreme Adventure

The Sharp Empire

The Sharp Empire II: The Serpent Strikes Back

The Sharp Empire III: The Phantom of the Galaxy

The Sharp Empire IV: Return of the Gospel

Coming Soon:

Whip 5: The Journey Across the Galaxy

Printed in the United States
By Bookmasters